Snow White

02/17

Illustrated by Beatriz Castro

Collins

Snow White and Rose Red were sisters, and twins at that, but they were as unalike as a pea and a peppercorn. Snow White was a pale, quiet girl, who liked reading. Rose Red had freckles and red hair, and was sporty, brave and full of bright ideas. In spite of their differences – or perhaps because of them – they made a splendid team.

Their mother had named them Blanche and Scarlet when they were born. But their father changed them to Snow White and Rose Red for a joke one day, and the names had stuck, as they often do.

But their father had long since died, so now they lived with their mother and their dog, Mr Henshaw, in a small house in a town, like you and me. Between them they could cook and mend things and tell stories, and that, really, is all you need in life.

One night, Snow White was telling a particularly tall tale about a monkey that went to the moon. She was just getting to the good bit with the alien, when there was a loud knock at the door.

"I'll go," said Rose Red, "in case it's an alien, or a monkey!"

Snow White rolled her eyes, because she knew aliens were just made up, and monkey's paws too soft to knock that hard.

4

When Rose Red opened the door, the sisters were both surprised because there, on the doorstep of number 42, wasn't an alien, or a monkey. But a bear. An enormous, hairy bear.

And what's more, he could talk.

"Hello," he said. "It's awfully cold out. May I come in?"

Now Rose Red knew that bears were dangerous, but she could also see that this one was shivering. Besides, she knew how to outsmart a bear if she needed, so she let him in.

"Come and sit by the fire," said Rose Red, making Mr Henshaw budge up on the big chair.

The bear sat down on the big chair. Mr Henshaw sat on the bear.

"I was just telling a story," said Snow White.

"Oh, I'm terrific at stories," said the bear.
"Can I tell one? Can I?"

He seemed so keen that Snow White and Rose Red could only nod.

So the bear told them a tale about his home in the woods, and the awful dwarf who lived underneath it. "And when the mud thaws in spring, he climbs up through his burrow and tries to steal my treasure."

"That's terrible," said Rose Red, though she knew in her heart that a bear couldn't own any treasure.

"Horrible," agreed Snow White, wondering how a bear could think up such an extraordinary story.

"Well, I should go now," said the bear, who'd warmed up by then. "But perhaps I'll see you tomorrow."

"I hope so," said Snow White.

"Me too," said Rose Red.

And they weren't disappointed. Because, night after
night, the bear came and told them the same tall tale
about his treasure, and the awful dwarf who'd steal it
in the spring.

Then spring came.

"This will be my last visit," said the bear, "because now I've got a job to do."

"Do you have to protect your treasure from the awful dwarf?" guessed Snow White.

"I do," said the bear. "I do!"

The girls hugged the bear and smiled at his fib, even though they were very sad he was leaving.

"Maybe he'll be back tomorrow," said Rose Red.

"Of course," said Snow White, who always had hope
in her heart.

But the bear didn't come back tomorrow, or the day
after that or the day after that.

For three whole weeks, the girls and Mr Henshaw
waited, but still the bear didn't come.

"Well, there's only one thing for it," said Rose Red to her sister one fine May morning. "We're going on a bear hunt."

Snow White knew better than to argue with Rose Red when she was in that sort of mood, so she found her rucksack and packed them each a sandwich, a bottle of water and an apple. Then off they set with Mr Henshaw to find the bear.

They didn't have to go far
before they found something.
But it wasn't a bear.
It was a small man with
an enormous beard, who
seemed to be stuck in
a crack in a rock.

"Help me," he begged.
"If you do, I'll give you
the treasure that's inside
this hole."

"What sort of treasure?"
asked Snow White.

"Gold," said the small man.
"Also a dried starfish,
a yoyo and
a chocolate raisin."

"OK," said Snow White,
who was keen on starfish.

"Fine," said Rose Red,
who liked yoyos more
than anything.

14

So between them they heaved and they hawed and they set the little man free. But no sooner was he released, than he ran off, taking all the treasure for himself.

"How rude," said Rose Red.

"I've a funny feeling," said Snow White. "I don't think that was just any little man with a big beard. I think that was the awful dwarf, and he was stealing the bear's treasure."

"Oh, my!" exclaimed Rose Red. "You're right."

The sisters were shocked at their mistake. The bear had been telling the truth and, worse, they'd helped the dwarf to steal from their friend.

"But tomorrow's another day," said Snow White, calm as a cucumber. "And are you thinking what I'm thinking?"

"I believe I am," said Rose Red.

And she was. Because, while the sisters were different in lots of small ways, they'd one big thing in common: they both loved the bear and would do whatever it took to help him.

So the very next day, off they went again with their
lunch and Mr Henshaw, ready to put their plan
into action.

They didn't have to go far before they found the awful
dwarf again. This time, he had his hand stuck in
the hollow of a tree.

"Help me," he begged. "If you do, I'll give you
the treasure that's inside this hole."

"What sort of treasure?" asked Snow White.

"Gold," said the small man. "Also a plastic hippo,
a spinning top, and a stick of bubble gum."

"OK," said Snow White, although she didn't care for
bubble gum.

"Fine," said Rose Red, who'd never liked spinning tops.

So once more they heaved and they hawed and they set
the dwarf free. But this time, instead of letting him go,
Rose Red sat down on his chest so he couldn't move, and
Snow White tied his hands and feet with a skipping rope
she carried in her rucksack for emergencies.

"That should do it," she said.

"How dare you!" shrieked the awful dwarf, who was
crosser than ever. "You're only children, and smelly
ones at that!"

21

"Now, now," said Rose Red. "There's no need to be rude."

"Although the more noise you make, the better," said Snow White, and gave a yell of her own. "Bear!" she shouted. "Come quick, Bear!"

"Bear?" wailed the awful dwarf.

"Oh, yes," said Rose Red. "He's our friend. Didn't we tell you?" And she yelled for the bear, too.

They yelled and they yelled until they both had sore throats.

"Ha! He's not coming," laughed the dwarf.
"He's not your friend at all."

But the dwarf was wrong. Because at that
very moment, from behind an enormous
oak tree, appeared the bear.

"Girls!" he exclaimed.
"And Mr Henshaw too.
What a lovely surprise."

23

"Bear!" replied Snow White, happily.

"Bear!" repeated Rose Red, joyfully.

"Bear?" cried the dwarf, who wasn't happy or joyful. "Run for your lives!"

But the girls didn't run. And, of course, the dwarf couldn't run.

"Why aren't you scared?" he asked, trembling. "Look at his terrible teeth and his terrible claws!"

"We aren't scared because we can see what you can't," said Snow White. "That this bear has a warm heart and a kind soul."

"Unlike you," said Rose Red. "Your heart is cold and your soul is weak."

"And besides," said Snow White, "he's our friend."

24

At those last three words, an incredible thing happened. There was a puff of smoke and a smell a bit like burnt fishfingers, and the bear turned into a boy. And not just any boy, but a prince! Though not an especially handsome one. Just an average prince, with an average fortune.

"Yikes!" said Snow White.

"Crikey!" said Rose Red.

"No, my name's Dave, actually," said the prince. "Thank you. This dwarf killed my parents and turned me into a bear. He cursed me to remain like that forever unless someone said they'd be my friend. But who could be friends with an enormous bear?"

"We could," said Rose Red and Snow White together.

And the sisters threw their arms round Dave and gave him an enormous bear hug.

So now Dave lives with Snow White and Rose Red and their mother and Mr Henshaw. However, there've been some changes at number 42 ...

There's an ivory-coloured tower for Snow White to read in.

A climbing wall for Rose Red.

And lamb chops every Sunday for Mr Henshaw.

But they all still sit by the fire every night and tell tall tales.

And the girls still mend everything, because Dave is useless with a hammer or a saw (although he does make a mean raspberry mousse).

And as for the dwarf? I think he's still waiting for someone to untie him.

The bear's tale

Ideas for reading

Written by Clare Dowdall, PhD
Lecturer and Primary Literacy Consultant

Reading objectives:
- increase familiarity with a wide range of books including fairy stories and retell orally
- discuss words and phrases that capture the reader's interest and imagination
- draw inferences and justify these with evidence
- make predictions from details stated and applied

Spoken language objectives:
- participate in discussions, presentations, performances, role play, improvisations and debates

Curriculum links: PSHE family relationships

Resources: digital cameras; art materials (pens, paper, paint)

Build a context for reading
- Ask children what they know about Snow White and Rose Red. What kind of characters are they?
- Look at the front cover and read the blurb. Challenge children to make predictions about what will happen in the story.
- Discuss where this traditional tale might come from. Ask children what features traditional tales sometimes have (talking animals, magical events, mysterious creatures, happy endings).

Understand and apply reading strategies
- Read pp2–3 together. Help children to develop understanding and make inferences by looking closely at the language used, e.g. What does "In spite of their differences – or perhaps because of them – they made a splendid team" tell the children about Rose Red and Snow White's relationship?